'Get down off that statue!
Get off that horse!' shouted Fred.

1

Rocky jumped down.
The others ran off and Rocky followed.

2

Later Rocky lay in bed but
he could not forget the statue.
What was that strange sound?

Rocky looked out of his window.
The statue was moving.
It came over the grass in the Square.
It was the Duke on his horse.

The horse came to a stop outside his window.
The Duke looked up at Rocky.
'Quick, jump down,' he said.

Rocky shut his eyes and jumped.
He dropped onto the horse.
'Good,' said the Duke.

Rocky opened his eyes and looked around.
The Square was not there.
He was on a hill.

There were men all around.
They had red coats and guns.

Rocky jumped off the horse.
'Give this boy a coat and a drum,'
said the Duke.

Rocky put on the coat and picked up the drum.
'Play the drum when I shout,' said the Duke.

The Duke put up his hand.
'Quick march!' he shouted.
The men began to march.

Rocky played his drum.
Rat-a-tat-tat.
Rat-a-tat-tat it went.

12

Rat-a-tat-tat.
Rat-a-tat-tat.

The Duke smiled at Rocky.
'Keep it up,' he said.
Rat-a-tat-tat went the drum.

Rocky played his drum.
But what was that other sound?
It was his mother.
'Wake up!' she said.

His mother was there by the bed.
'Wake up, Rocky!' she said.
'Are you going to lie in bed all day?'